SCARY SHORT STORIES FOR TEENS
BOOK 1

A COLLECTION OF BONE CHILLING, CREEPY, HORROR SHORT STORIES

BRYCE NEALHAM

CONTENTS

STORY 1

BOY WITH THE RED SHIRT

In the late fall of 2009 I was driving my friend's home after a night of beer and bowling. I was a designated driver and I was as sober as a surgeon.

We were taking back roads to avoid the road works on the highways and driving through mostly small residential areas and wide open patches of farmland.

Less than a mile away from the first stop where I would be dropping off one of my friends I spotted something on the side of the road. I applied the brakes and slowed down.

There in the pitch darkness was a young boy just wandering down the road all by himself. He was maybe about 7 or 8 years old. I pulled off to the side of the road and quickly got out and walked over to him.

He paused when he saw me coming and just nervously stared at me like a kitten would look at you from a cage in a pet store. It was evident that he had been crying.

I told him my name and asked him if he was alright, why he was out here and where he was going. He was wearing a red polo shirt that was about two sizes too large, green shorts and flip-flops.

The poor guy was probably very cold although he was doing a great job of not showing it. After hesitating a few heartbeats he said his name was Simon and he had run away from home, gotten

1

lost and couldn't find his way back. He spoke in a kind of shaky monotone whisper like he was worried that he would say something wrong and I would abandon him on the side of the road.

I asked where he lived and he gave me an address. Right away I pulled out my cell phone and asked for his parent's number so I could call them and he claimed that he couldn't remember it.

At this time from behind me my rowdy drunken friends were being obnoxious and loud and calling out questions to me from back in the car like what the kids deal was and how long we would be parked there.

My buddy in the front seat got out of the car to take a leak in the weeds. I turned back to the boy and told him that I would take him home. I reached out to take his hand but he ignored me and walked right past towards the car.

I figured he must be in shock and so I let him climb into the now vacant passenger seat and I told my drunken friend who got out of the car to climb into the hatchback.

I closed the passenger door once the kid was inside. He didn't put on his seatbelt but I didn't force him to either. I didn't want to make him feel like I was abducting him or tying him down, I just wanted him to remain calm.

I put the car into drive and pulled back out into the street going exactly the speed limit. All of my intoxicated friends were awkwardly introducing themselves from the backseat but the boy just stared ahead with his eyes never leaving the dashboard in front of him.

I noticed after a few moments he started crying again. I couldn't tell if these were tears of pain, shame or fear.

"Are you alright?" I asked him. He nodded and let out a tiny hiccup. I told him that there were some fast food napkins under the seat and he reached down and used them to wipe out his eyes.

I considered calling the cops but one of my drunken friends was underage and I had the feeling that the police would be more interested in them than the kid.

I decided to drop off my two friends first just so the kid felt less overwhelmed and then I would make a detour to where the kid said his house was.

After another 10 minutes I had dropped off two of my three friends and the last one had fallen asleep in the backseat. I left the residential side streets and got back onto the main roads. I drove for a few minutes before finding the street I wanted.

I asked the kid, "How long were you walking?"

The kid just stared ahead and replied, "A long time".

After some time I eventually found the road I was looking for. I pulled into the cul-de-sac and drove to the very last house. It was tucked away behind some trees.

I pulled into the driveway but before I could even park the car the kid opened the door and hopped out. "Thanks!" he called out. I remember thinking that his voice sounded so much more cheerful and calm than it had before. He ran towards the house where there were absolutely no lights on and he waved to me.

Once he got to the front porch I leaned over to pull the passenger door shut and was surprised to find the handle was icy cold to the touch. Not so cold that it was unpleasant, just very chilled like it had spent a few minutes in a freezer.

When I looked back up the kid was gone. I hadn't heard the door open or shut. No lights had come on inside the house either. I waited for another half-minute but my friend's snoring in the back reminded me that I needed to get him home.

After I dropped my last passenger off I parked my car and decided to call the police just to perform a welfare check on the kid. I gave the operator the address and after a moment she informed me that no one was listed as a living there.

Confused, I told her what had happened and asked her to send a patrol car to meet me there because I was afraid that the kid may have just been squatting alone in the property.

It was past 2 a.m. when I pulled into that driveway again. Two police cars were already there waiting for me. They said they had swept the entire property and checked the inside of the house but there was no one there.

Apparently, the year before there had been a terrible fire in the kitchen that destroyed most of the ground floor and half of the second floor above it. The house was uninhabitable and the current owners were in a battle with the insurance company over what to do with it.

I told them about the boy and they responded that if he had been there he was long gone now.

A few days later I decided to do some digging to find out what really went on in that house. After spending an hour or so researching online I discovered that several years prior to the fire another family had lived in the house.

They had lost a son in a freak accident. He had been killed while riding his bike on the side of the road. The spot where he died was the exact spot where I had found Simon.

The boy's name was Robin but he also had a middle name which just happened to be, Simon. At that moment I felt like I had swallowed wet cement.

I refused to believe that I encountered anything paranormal. The boy had been solid, made of flesh and bone but even as I told myself that I remembered that I had never actually touched him.

A couple of weeks later I drove by the same spot where I found him just to get a look at the place in daylight. After idling in my car for a few moments I drove off.

STORY 2

THEY WERE NOT FRIENDLY

This story took place when I was only a teenager. I lived with my two parents, my brother and sister and my grandmother. I had a younger sister too but she and my grandfather both died in a car accident several years earlier.

We moved houses not long after the accident. Our new house was much bigger but still had a cozy feel to it.

One Halloween, our whole family gathered in the living room where we had lit a fire and put a movie on for the evening. Grandma stayed upstairs in her bedroom because she was feeling tired and just wanted to read and relax.

It was late and trick-or-treaters started to thin out. We were about 30 minutes into the movie when we heard a shriek from upstairs. It was grandma. Instantly we all ran upstairs in a panic.

As we climbed the stairs we could hear sobbing and grandma saying, "It's you…it's really you!"

She kept repeating it in a kind of hoarse cry as we made our way to her room. Once inside we noticed grandma had fallen down onto the floor with her back against the wall. She looked paler than any of us had ever seen her before and her expression was a mixture of bliss and excitement.

Standing across the room dressed in an old-fashioned suit with a hat in his hands stood my grandfather.

We were all stunned and totally speechless. Had I known what I know now, I would have ordered him out of our house that very minute, but I didn't.

My mom was the first one to break down; seeing her father again was just too much for her. My grandfather simply smiled and reassured her.

Grandma proceeded to tell us what happened. She was in her room getting ready for bed when she heard tapping on the window. When she turned she saw grandpa peeking at her.

She explained this wasn't the first time something like this had happened. When you lose someone you see them everywhere, but when grandpa didn't leave and motioned her over to the window she knew this time it was different. Grandma opened the window and let grandpa in.

My grandfather spoke to us and shared stories of the other side. He mentioned how beautiful it is and how all of your wildest dreams can't compare to the reality of it.

I was skeptical, but I was just so happy to see my grandpa that I ignored my inner skeptic. He explained how when the time is right spirits can come back to the land of the living.

He apologized for not visiting sooner, claiming he had tried many times but that he simply hadn't been experienced enough until this year. We all believed him of course.

Once all of this had finished we agreed that it was best if we left my grandparents alone to catch up. My grandpa turned to my grandmother and reached out his hand.

"I've got a lot to tell you, come with me" he smiled as he said this; a warm friendly smile.

She took his hand and together they walked down the hall and out of sight. The rest of us went back downstairs, still shaken up by what had occurred.

We spent a long time in silence there by the fire. Trick-or-treaters would stop by even more infrequently than before. Eventually we got back to talking and joking almost as though there wasn't a ghost upstairs

It was the best night we spent together in years. At around 11pm the doorbell rang. We weren't expecting any more children, especially this late.

A cry of "trick-or-treat" came from outside the front door so my mom went to the door. She swung it open. My mother froze. Right there on the doorstep was a young girl wearing a pink princess outfit.

"What's wrong mommy?" the girl asked.

My father and my older siblings looked at each other before racing to the front door. When we got there my heart leaped into my throat and tears filled my eyes. Standing in the doorway was my younger sister, Sara. Sara had been killed in the car crash with grandpa years earlier.

If you have shared a house with a young child, then you know how deeply their absence is felt. There's no aspect of life they don't affect in one way or another and when Sara died nothing was the same. Now, there she stood, not a day older, not a mark on her body.

I broke down crying. When I looked around I saw that all my family was crying and Sara looked deeply troubled by it all.

"Did I do something wrong mommy?" she asked.

9

"Of course not honey", my mother replied. "We have all just missed you so much".

Sara came in the house and we all sat down talking. She was just the same as she had been back then. Our conversations went on for around 30 minutes when Sara looked towards my parents.

"Mom, dad can I show you something?" she asked.

"Of course you can, sweetheart," my mother said, still with tears in her eyes.

Sara leapt off the couch, "Great! Come with me!"

She grabbed both my parent's hands. Right at that moment I suddenly realized my grandma was still upstairs and she had no idea that Sara had come back.

So I went upstairs to get her. I got to the top of the stairs and saw my grandfather coming out of grandma's room quietly and shutting the door behind him.

When I asked him where grandma was he told me that she was resting. I asked if she could come downstairs and he simply said that wasn't possible. He also added that grandma would have plenty of time to spend with Sara.

I got excited, "Does this mean that you and Sara are staying for good?"

My grandfather just smiled and went downstairs with me. My older siblings were chatting in the living room when Sara came skipping in from around the corner all alone.

"Where's mom and dad?" I asked.

Sara looked up at me and smiled, "Well, when we went down to the basement they started kissing and hugging and told me to go upstairs, so I did."

That didn't sound right. I couldn't imagine my mother leaving Sara's side for a moment tonight. Nobody else seemed to find this strange though.

Grandpa just laughed and said that adults were weird and I would understand someday. He then turned to my brother and said he had brought a gift with him, something to make up for all the lost birthdays and Christmases.

He held out his hand for my brother to take. "Come with me," he said.

It was only at that point I suddenly grew suspicious. I asked my grandpa where the gift was, to which he simply replied, "Oh don't you worry, you'll get yours soon enough."

I urged my brother not to go with him, but he didn't listen taking my grandfather's hand. The two of them went down the hall together.

Sara turned to us and said, "Mommy and daddy have been down there for a while, let's go check on them." She reached out for my other sister, Meg.

"Come with me."

Meg reached for Sara and I slapped her hand away. "Don't go with her!" I shouted.

Meg ignored my outburst and took Sara's hand. The two of them went downstairs to the basement.

Grandpa came up to me, his eyes met mine, "I've got your gift ready now Billy. Come with me."

I ran past him into my room and shut the door behind me. I didn't know what to do. I didn't have a cell phone yet and there were no home phones in my room.

All I could do was sit there and wait for them to either break in or leave. Heavy footsteps came down the hall and just stopped outside my door. My grandfather began calling me, begging me to come out so he'd give me my present.

A few minutes later his voice was joined with Sara asking me to come out and play with her.

"Why don't you love me anymore Billy?" she cried.

I can't possibly tell you how hard it was to stay in there listening to my little sister begging me to play with her one last time, but the survival instinct was a strong one and I kept the door shut.

The clock chimed twelve and all fell silent. I looked under the door and my grandfather's figure was no longer cast in a shadow underneath.

I placed my ear to the door listening carefully and heard nothing. My family was out there possibly hurt; I had to go check or call for help or do something at least.

I took a deep breath to steady myself and opened the door. The hallway was empty. Across the hall through the open door I could see my brother laying there on the ground motionless. He was pale and didn't look like he was breathing.

I ran over to him and checked his wrist and his neck for a pulse but found nothing. All I saw was that one of his hands was tinged black, like it had been dipped in tar.

I ran upstairs and found my grandma in the same state; pale not breathing with her hands blackened.

My heart was racing, I had to go to the basement but I couldn't go because I knew what I would find there; the rest of my family lying pale and motionless dead. I sat there for a long time paralyzed before I decided I had to know.

The descent to the basement felt longer than it ever had before. It felt cold and each step felt like an eternity but when I got to the bottom I saw exactly what I knew I would find; my parents and my older sister laying on the floor.

I began to cry like I hadn't done since the day my little sister and grandpa died.

Suddenly I heard a sinister voice, "You stupid boy".

The voice was evil sounding just like every demon from every horror movie you have ever seen and worse.

I spun around and Sara was there, but she was different. Her eye sockets were empty, her mouth was a black lipless hole filled with fangs.

"You have no more family, no more loved ones. They are now mine and you will live the rest of your life alone."

I continued to stare at this creature before me, totally stunned and in shock.

It continued, "You will die somewhere all alone and afraid and you will never see your family again…ever!"

Then the thing paused and held out its hand, "Unless you come with me. You can be with all of us again, forever."

I'd like to tell you that I kept my distance, that I told her to get out of my house but what she said was true. I felt it deep in my bones; I'll never see my family again if I didn't go with her.

I was just a kid, a scared stupid kid who wanted his mom. I stood shakily and reached out my hands. Slowly, Sara's mouth formed a smile as I approached.

Then there was a noise upstairs, the clock chimed one o'clock. I looked up just for a heartbeat, there was a distant scream and when I looked forward Sara was gone.

I called the police. An investigation took place but nothing was ever really explained or resolved. I ended up living with my aunt and uncle in another state.

Years later, as an adult, I sold the house and everything in it and moved to a small apartment using the proceeds to put myself through school once I graduated.

This Halloween, if you see a loved one who passed away, please don't let them into your home. Don't take their hand and never go with them.

STORY 3

SHADOW THINGS

This happened about ten years ago when I was 13. My bedroom was in the loft of the house and so my parents had it refurbished as an extra bedroom.

One night I found that I just couldn't get to sleep. For whatever reason, I just suddenly didn't feel tired anymore.

Because my room was in the loft it would always be pitch black at night, especially with my door was closed. I didn't have any night lights and no other devices were on. I rolled over onto my side facing towards the wall and closed my eyes to at least attempt to get back to sleep.

A few minutes went by and I was still wide awake. I was beginning to get frustrated because I still couldn't fall asleep. Just as I was thinking about this I got the feeling that I wasn't alone anymore.

You know how you can just tell when someone's walked into the room, almost like the energy or density changes? Well, I had an older sister, Hannah, who had a habit of creeping into my room late at night to steal my stuff so I thought it's probably her.

I opened my eyes. My room was still dark which indicated to me that Hannah was not in the room because whenever she comes in she'd leave the door open a crack to let the hallway light in. Plus, she's incredibly loud, but this time my room was dead silent.

As soon as this realization dawned on me an overwhelming sense of dread came over me. I knew someone was in the room with me just as I know my own name, but since the human mind needs tangible proof of everything I decided to check…just in case I was imagining it.

If you know anything about loft beds, you know those things are loud when you move because you're basically propped up on stilts in the air. So as I moved, I tried to do so as quietly as possible so that whatever was in the room with me wasn't aware I was there.

By now I was pretty certain it wasn't just me in this room. I slowly sat up on the bed and looked across the room. Sure enough, there was this black figure in the shape of a person standing in front of my dresser.

I had a sudden feeling, a sense that whoever or whatever stood over there was evil. A malevolence practically oozed from it and spread over my bedroom.

This shape was literally blacker than the darkness of my bedroom. Imagine being in a pitch-black room then a figure materializes; no tangible features just a straight-up filled in outline in the shape of a person that is darker than the dark. That's what this thing was.

I don't know how but as soon as I laid my eyes on this thing I saw it turn its head and look at me. It didn't have any features so I didn't physically see its eyes looking at me but it's almost like I could feel it in my mind. It paralyzed me.

It began moving and walking towards my bunk bed ladder like it was going to climb up. I shot straight up in terror, knowing that if this thing got to me something bad was sure to happen, and reached over to turn on my ceiling fan light.

Luckily it was literally less than a foot away from where I was. I yelled out the guardian angel prayer that my parents taught me to say each and every day.

My mouth stumbled over the words with my haste and as soon as I finished I felt this overwhelming sense of peace and love come over me like I've never felt before. It was as if something was there protecting me.

When that feeling came, all sense of darkness and negativity just shattered. I was so calm and at peace. The dark figure had disappeared.

I was so calm that I just flicked the light back off and instantly fell asleep. I haven't seen a shadow person since that night but I regularly feel a "presence" in my room.

I would feel "something" standing near my bed at night. I'd wake me up, but I'll never see anything. Even now, as an adult, whenever I get scared I call for my guardian angel. It helps...sometimes.

STORY 4

HORROR HOUSE

When I was 16 I got a job as a personal assistant cleaning lady for a very wealthy couple who live in a big beautiful mansion on Lake Michigan.

It was a great job at the time but after a while I had to quit because of all the bad stuff that happened.

I made $12 an hour as a teenage girl which was a pretty good wage at the time, but now I know it's because the homeowners couldn't get anyone to stay and work for them.

I didn't see the owners all that much during the school year so I was happy to work 40-hour weeks in the summer and part-time while I was in school.

I would be left alone to clean the house and I had a key alarm code as well as gate codes so I could let myself in and out.

In the summer months I had help from a few other employees but in the school year I didn't. The place was absolutely gorgeous. I'd always open all the curtains to let the sun in and blast the surround sound speakers while I cleaned.

It wasn't until I was by myself that I started noticing how weird the place was. Nothing ever exactly felt welcoming about the place. Sure, it was pretty to look at but it was modern and everything was hard marble stone; not very homely in my opinion.

Anyway, my first experience happened when I was cleaning one day in silence. I remember specifically not turning on the music because I had a bad headache that day.

All of a sudden I heard loud music playing in the upstairs part of the house. Someone had turned on the music system.

The speaker system is controlled by a touchpad in the kitchen. When turned on, it would play music throughout the house besides the basement and master bedroom.

To play music in those areas you have to use the touchpad to sync it up with the rest of the house. The reason this whole thing was so alarming was because I was the only person in the house.

I walked upstairs to go check out what was going on and figured out why the music turned on by itself. I looked around and called out the home owner's names. Maybe they came in without me noticing or something, but the doors were all still locked and no one was home.

I shut off the music and went back downstairs not thinking much of it. Then, strange things began to happen. I'd be listening to music and it would suddenly turn it off or would be off and would turn on in a completely different area of the house.

I brushed it off as a faulty wire or something and didn't think much of it.

Another time, I was cleaning the workout room in their basement. I never wanted to go in this room and I really couldn't tell you why; something about it was weird. It was always super cold, even after I would turn the heating up, and dark and I just felt really anxious in that room.

I definitely tried to avoid it as best I could but my boss would get mad when dust would build up, so I forced myself to go in there once a week to tidy up.

So, I was in the workout room using a broom and a mop to clean the floors. I remember sweeping up the floor and propping the broom against one of the workout machines while I used the mop.

Suddenly, the broom tipped over, hitting the wall then the baseboard and then the floor; making three distinct knocks.

What I heard after that scared me so badly that I refused to go into the room by myself ever again.

Immediately following the knocks made by the broom falling, three knocks responded in the exact same knocking pattern. Knock, knock, knock.

These knocks came from inside the walls of the gym. It was not an echo nor was it a scared animal. It was deliberate knocking.

I was completely alone in a big, quiet house in the middle of nowhere and someone was knocking back at me from inside the wall.

STORY 5

CAT DEMON

I was around 28 years old. I had been married for two years and had two kids. I was a stay at home mom and my husband worked as a landscaper. We lived in a double-wide modular home.

One night I was home alone because the kids were visiting their grandmother and I decided to relax and watch a movie.

Our home was about a mile away from the nearest neighbor and it rested atop a large hill that was surrounded by a dense forest.

I had barely started the movie when I heard what sounded like a kitten meowing outside. I got up and decided to investigate. I went outside and immediately noticed something wasn't right because the meowing sounded like it was coming from about 20 feet up in a large oak tree.

When I walked over and stood directly underneath the branches the meowing turned into a deep growling…almost like a lion or some other big cat.

It was too dark out to see anything clearly. Deeply unsettled by this, I went back inside and locked the door while I contemplated whether or not I would be overreacting by calling the cops.

I then heard a loud boom on my roof followed by the most insane high-pitched scream I had ever heard. I covered my ears, ran to the bedroom and grabbed the shotgun from the closet.

I was shaking with fear. I felt in the air that something was different, something was not normal. I called my husband at work and just as he answered the screeching sound started up again only this time it was deeper and longer.

My husband told me to hang up and call the police but I knew they wouldn't arrive for at least an hour so instead I decided to stand facing the bay window with my shotgun up and ready.

After a few moments I saw what looked like an emaciated teenager jump down in front of the window and face my direction. He had completely white glowing eyes as well as white hair and extremely pale skin.

He looked up as if he was sniffing the air, then he growled while glaring at me. His eyes seemed to get brighter as he did so.

After another moment he opened his mouth and revealed what appeared to be a forked tongue. Before I could even process what I was looking at I heard more footsteps on the roof. Suddenly, a small girl that looked just like him jumped down from above, also looking directly at me with glowing white eyes.

I instinctively cocked back the hammer on the shotgun and pointed it at them both. I didn't want to shoot through the window if I could help it but I wasn't going to let them get in. They pressed their faces to the window and all I could think about was how silent it was all of a sudden and how pulling the trigger would break the silence.

I'm not sure how long we locked eyes but I suddenly noticed a pair of headlights coming up the driveway and I recognized a police car. I wanted to scream out to him not to get out of the car but before I could even open my mouth both white eyed creatures leapt into the darkness of my garden.

The policeman never caught a glimpse of them and ultimately didn't believe me. My husband's mother did and confided in me that she had seen them before. She believed that they were some kind of demon.

Over the next few years before we moved away I would occasionally hear meowing from the trees around my house at night but I would never go out to investigate.

I'm not sure what they were, but paranormal or not I don't ever want to find out what they wanted from me.

STORY 6

SNOWSTORM CABIN

My name is Thomas and I'm a photographer. I took a trip last year with my wife to the Colorado Mountains for an art project. My wife is also an avid skier so she talked me into adding skiing into the trip.

We had the option to book a room at a ski resort or rent out a private log cabin. The second option seemed more romantic so I picked that one, plus it didn't hurt that it was cheaper.

The cabin was nothing luxurious; it was a single floor four room cozy little thing. It had a two-person bedroom, a small living room, a kitchen and a bathroom.

They may have been small but the actual idea of being secluded in a warm log cabin during a blizzard was amazing. However, the storm was interfering with the cable signal so we didn't have much to do.

This one particular evening it was just starting to get dark out but there was still a decent amount of light outside, so I thought it would be perfect for getting a few shots and videos in the blizzard for backgrounds and wallpapers.

I told my wife I'd be back within 10 minutes and slipped on my boots and coat. The moment I stepped outside and shut the door I noticed footsteps leading up to the door in the snow that had blown under the wooden awning.

I could see the prints doubled as whoever left them there, turned and went the opposite direction.

I was freaked out but I wasn't about to go inside and scare my wife so I decided to give in to my curiosity and followed the prints.

To the right side of the cabin right away I noticed that they led to the bedroom window. My heart froze in fear when I saw this. I could see my wife sitting on the bed using her iPad. She noticed me outside through the window waved at me.

I waved back and then continued to follow the footprints around the cabin to the other side. They led to the living room window on the other side. Someone was stalking us!

How long had we been watched by this mysterious person? I found myself standing there for a good minute asking myself if I should follow the footprints anymore. For whatever reason, I decided I would.

They were now leading away from the cabin. I continued to follow the prints and they lead me to an opening into the trees. That was where I saw him.

I saw a man wearing a black coat facing a tree. He was slouched down looking at the ground; still as a statue. I could see the snow piling up on his hood and shoulders as though he had been there, unmoving for a long while.

I froze in my tracks trying not to make a sound. I would have asked him if he needed help but there was something about the way he just stood there that gave me the creeps.

He stood there, not doing anything. I then heard him giggling. It was no ordinary giggle...it sounded evil. The giggling got louder and he began to sound like some kind of deranged freak.

I started to gradually move backwards without even turning around making sure this man didn't turn around or notice me. When I got at a visual distance I turned around and stomped through the snow back to the cabin.

I slammed the door shut and my wife came over to see what was wrong. I saw worry in her eyes; I guess she saw the worry on my face and knew I had seen something.

I told her what I saw and she immediately started packing her things telling me we're leaving right away. I told her, no we're not going anywhere because I would not get a refund for leaving the cabin early. I wasn't about to up and leave just because some weird guy was walking around outside.

She made a point of locking both bolts on the door and making sure all the windows were sealed shut. For the rest of the night we stayed close together until it was time for bed.

"What if he's still out there?" I remember my wife asking me.

"There's no way he's still out there, its -10 degrees!" I assured her.

Listening to the wind blowing outside along with the small flakes of snow hitting the windows was strangely relaxing and I knew we would be able to fall asleep quickly. Before we could, there was a knock at the bedroom window.

We were both still awake and we both knew it was a knock from a person. I ushered my wife out of bed and out into the living room without turning on any lights.

There was nothing in the cabin to use as a weapon whatsoever; our only option was to run before something horrendous happened.

I told my wife we'd have to forget our luggage and make a dash for the Jeep. We slipped on our boots and coats in the dark in a matter of seconds but then we heard a knock at the living room window from the opposite side of the cabin.

We took that opportunity to unbolt and run out the front door. As I ran I pressed the Jeep's remote unlock button and we hopped in the Jeep. I put the key in the ignition and turned it. It started with ease.

As soon as the headlights flashed on, we could see the man standing facing the log cabin. He stood totally still just facing the wall of the cabin in the same position I had seen him in earlier as if he were hiding his face.

I got the Hell out of there and drove nonstop to the nearby ski resort. We stayed there for the night and went back the next day to the log cabin to collect our things. We never saw that guy again.

STORY 7

THE CRANKING FLASHLIGHT

I'll never forget the time me and my brother snuck out past our bedtime to explore an allegedly haunted house down the block.

I was only 10 and my brother Robert was only 12. When our parents said good night to us I went to Robert's room to prepare for our adventure.

We took a couple of hand-powered flashlights with us and hopped outside through the window; his room was on the first floor.

Those hand powered flashlights worked by constantly pushing in a little trigger that would create light inside the lens, they were noisy as hell but they were convenient.

Once we were outside we just walked down the block and in two minutes we were there. It was rumored by all the neighborhood kids and teens that the place was haunted.

Everything about it was creepy. The old antique design of the house, the isolation from the rest of the houses, and the broken windows and rotting wood...it all seemed perfect for a horror movie.

We went around to the backyard but the door was locked. I felt a bit of relief thinking we might just go home because I was starting to get scared already, but my brother made a shocking move next.

He grabbed a plank of wood lying in the grass and began smashing the already chipped window. Eventually there was enough of an opening to unlock it and slide it up completely.

We hopped inside and began cranking those noisy flashlights. Immediately after entering the house we both picked up on the fact that it was around 90 degrees in there. This was odd because it was a September night and outside was around the mid-70s.

There was no graffiti or anything anywhere, in fact it was relatively empty besides a few pieces of furniture that were clearly not worth taking.

It seemed we were the first to enter the house. We went upstairs to the main floor from the little den area and continued cranking the flashlights. That's when we heard the slightest crack in the floorboards from right above us.

We both jumped. I tugged for Robert to leave but he told me the place is old as hell and that it's just house noises.

I stopped cranking the flashlight at this point and I urged Robert to do the same but he only called me stupid for suggesting something so ridiculous.

Then there was another crack in the floorboards from above us. Robert began walking upstairs. I didn't want to go up there but I was not about to stay downstairs alone.

I followed behind him as we both climbed the stairs. There was a door that led to a room right above where we were standing. I begged him not to open it but he must have just wanted to be the big tough older brother. He began to reach for the doorknob while still cranking the noisy flashlight, but then he stopped.

I was confused. I could see in the dark he was moving his ear up against the door listening for something. There was total silence. Then the most deafening nightmare-inducing moment of my life occurred.

A single bang on the door from the other side sent my brother staggering into the wall in pain covering his ear. We dropped the flashlights, ran downstairs and straight out the back door all the way home.

We were so loud when we got back that our parents found us out. We told them what happened but they naturally didn't care and grounded us both for a week.

Two nights later I woke to the sound of something from outside my window and a glare of brightness sneaking in through my slightly opened blind.

I sat up and my heart sank when I realized it was the sound of the crank to my flashlight. I stood up and looked out the window and that's when the sound stopped.

There was nothing but complete blackness out there. After that experience I woke the next day feeling very weak and in a low mood. My brother felt the same.

Whatever happened that night has stayed with my brother and I.

STORY 8

THE HITCHER

I've learned one thing from my one-and-only experience picking up a hitchhiker, don't pick up a hitchhiker.

It was a Saturday night, probably around 1:00 in the morning and I had just finished my late shift job at a pizza place.

I was driving down a road that I usually took to get into my town. It was a long stretch of nothing but woods on either side with the occasional residents.

As usual at this time of night, around our quiet old town, there was not a single other car on the road. I turned on the off-road lights on my Jeep to have optimal vision on the unlit highway.

Suddenly, I spotted somebody far down the road just standing at the side. As I got closer I saw him raise his arm up and stick up his thumb; he was trying to hitch a ride.

My heart started racing because I had no idea if I should stop or not. I slowed down just to get a better look at the guy before I made that decision.

He seemed like a young man, maybe 25 years old. He had on a light grey hoodie with the hood over his head and blue denim jeans.

The time to make a decision was immediate and with a lack of my better judgment in the heat of the moment I came to a stop.

I rolled down the window and asked him where he was heading.

35

"To visit a friend just up the road", he said in a deep quiet tone.

"Hop in", I called out the window.

He opened the door to my Jeep and stepped inside slowly. Jeep Wranglers have very tight seals on the doors so when he tried to close the door the first time it didn't shut.

I politely said, "Oh the door didn't shut, just open and slam it shut real hard because these doors are hard to close".

The body language he was giving off in response was unsettling. About three seconds after I had finished my sentence he looked at me then turned his head slowly to the right and again waited three or four more seconds before finally opening the door and then slamming it back shut.

By the way this guy was moving I already regretted my decision to let him in so I put my foot on the gas. We started moving along the road a lot faster. The speed limit on this road was 55 but I was going 75 just to get the guy to his destination quicker.

"So how far did you say you're going?" I asked.

There was an awkward gap of silence before he replied, "Just a few miles ahead".

I wanted to turn the radio on to kill this awkward and downright creepy silence but something in my head told me not to.

For whatever reason, suddenly I could see just through the corner of my eye that the man had turned his head and was staring in my direction. At this point I was telling myself that I needed to get this guy out of my car.

For a good mile I felt his gaze just hitting me like a brick and all the while I tried my best not to look back. Finally he turned his head the other way and said, "You know I've been wondering for the longest time if it's just worth it to end it all".

I looked at him in confusion. He dug his hand into his pocket and said, "I've been carrying this knife with me for the past few weeks wondering when the right time would come".

He pulled out a big red knife with a 6 inch blade from inside his jacket. At that instant I felt like my stomach had dropped out of my body.

I told him to put the knife away. He told me in a calm emotionless voice, "Pull over now, next to that sign". I did what he said coming to a stop next to a speed limit sign.

What followed still haunts me to this day. He began to slit his forearm next to three other scars from previous self-inflicted cuts. He let out a disturbing moan.

I managed to choke out the words, "You need to get out of my car right now buddy". He looked at me again and said, "Get out of the car; I want to show you something".

I told him no and he raised his knife up closer to me as an obvious threat.

"Just get out for a second, there's something I want to show you behind that sign".

I knew my life was on the line and I had to be smart. I said, "Yeah okay man, let's go".

I opened the door to my Jeep making a point of leaving it open. I raised my hands in the air and backed away slowly from the door. He also left the car and started walking over to my side.

At the exact moment that he was directly behind the car I jumped back in the driver's seat and threw the Jeep into drive.

I floored it down the road never looking back. I got back home within 10 minutes still breathing heavily and wanting to throw up.

This was the scariest thing that has ever happened to me and I urge you that if you by some chance see a hitchhiker on a dead road at some odd hours of the night…do not take any course of action other than speeding right past them!

STORY 9

THE PLAYGROUND

I'm a single father currently living with my five-year-old son. I have an old wooden playground in my backyard. It has a tire swing, monkey bars and a big slide.

A couple of times recently I've heard noises coming from the playground at night. I'll start from the first night.

I woke up one night last week to the sound of something squeaking from outside. I recognized it to be the sound of the rusty chain of the tire swing spinning around.

I also heard a young child's laughter out there. I thought it was my son so I went to his room to find him in his bed fast asleep.

Seeing him in his bed meant that some stranger was in my yard but when I opened the back door to the backyard there was no one back there. However, the tire swing was spinning slowly as if somebody had just gotten off of it.

I wasn't too panicked about it and figured it was probably some kid just sneaking into my yard. I decided to get back to sleep.

The next night I woke up again to the sound of someone stomping up and down the slide, once again accompanied by the sound of a child's laughter.

I checked my son's room to find him in bed. This was getting weird. This time I thought I'd be a little smarter about it and checked the window first before going outside.

Nothing was out there though, not on the playground at least. I still went outside anyway just to make sure.

For a couple nights after that, nothing happened and I completely forgot about it but on the third night while in bed a knock at my window startled me.

I sat up in shock for a good minute afraid to look outside but eventually I was brave enough to do so. I looked out the foggy window and through the smudge I could see both the swings on the swing set swinging lightly accompanied with the laughter of a child again.

I ran as fast as I could down those stairs and out the back door but instead of finding a couple of deviant little kids back there instead I saw a towering figure standing by the slide.

It was too dark outside to see any features but its form was almost inhuman. It was black, almost in shadow and it was at least 7 foot tall. It was also very thin and lanky. Whatever it was, I could feel it staring at me.

Fear took over me. I turned to run back inside making sure to lock the door behind me. I called the police.

The wait for an officer to arrive was the longest 20 minutes I'd ever experienced. By the time they got there though the figure on the playground was gone.

They took down what little information I could give them and left. I wish I could say that was the last occurrence, but just last night there was another knock in my window. I simply ignored it this time, though I'm dreading going to sleep tonight.

MORE BOOKS IN THE **CREEPY STORY HOUR** COLLECTION...

Scary Short Stories for Teens Book 2

Scary Short Stories for Teens Book 3

Made in the USA
Las Vegas, NV
19 September 2022